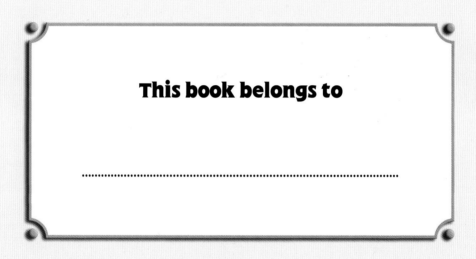

This book belongs to

....

Thomas the Tank Engine
Story Treasury

**A treasury of 12 favourite stories from the
Thomas Story Library Collection**

Thomas
the Tank Engine
Story Treasury

With 12 favourite stories

EGMONT

EGMONT

We bring stories to life

First published in Great Britain 2008
This edition published 2012
by Egmont UK Limited
239 Kensington High Street
London W8 6SA

Thomas the Tank Engine & Friends™

CREATED BY BRITT ALLCROFT

Based on the Railway Series by the Reverend W Awdry
© 2008 Gullane (Thomas) LLC. A HIT Entertainment company.
Thomas the Tank Engine & Friends and Thomas & Friends are trademarks of Gullane (Thomas) Limited.
Thomas the Tank Engine & Friends and Design is Reg. U.S. Pat. & Tm. Off.

978 0 603 56768 1
45878/4
Printed in China

contents

Thomas is a popular, cheeky little engine who is happiest in the thick of things in the yard. He often gets into scrapes, but only because he's so eager to be involved!

Bertie the bus has a lot in common with Thomas. Bertie's smile and ready-to-help attitude convinces the engines that sometimes – just sometimes – roads have their uses as well!

Cranky the Crane can be rather high and mighty, and loves to tease the engines. He can be very rude, but does as he is told in the end.

Gordon is the Big Express Engine. The fastest and most powerful of all the engines, he still finds time to help the smaller engines too.

Sir Topham Hatt, or **The Fat Controller** as his engines call him, went from being a young railway engineer to the Chairman of the Company. He is loved by everyone on Sodor.

Toby the tram engine is old-fashioned in his looks, but a very hard worker. Sometimes grumpy, he's always cheered up by his faithful coach, Henrietta.

Henry is a long, fast engine – even though he used not to be. He wasn't very well so was given a new shape and is now really fast!

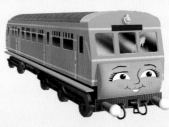

Daisy is lots of fun, but can think she's above some of the duties expected of a diesel railcar. The Fat Controller soon brings her into line!

Diesel was the first diesel engine to arrive on Sodor. He likes to play tricks on the steam engines who know just how troublesome he can be!

Emily is a beautiful engine with shiny paintwork and gleaming brass fittings. She's also very brave, and loves to help others!

Donald and Douglas are twin tender engines from Scotland. The Fat Controller saved them from being scrapped, so they are very grateful to him.

Percy is the junior member of the engine team. Always keen to help, the other engines can take advantage of his nice nature, but he never really minds!

Thomas and the New Branch Line

This is a story about Thomas the Tank Engine.
Thomas worked really hard, shunting
coaches for the big engines.

But what he wanted more than anything
was his very own branch line . . .

Thomas the Tank Engine had six small wheels, a short stumpy funnel, a short stumpy boiler and a short stumpy dome. He was a fussy little engine, always pulling coaches about.

He pulled them to the station ready for the big engines to take out on journeys; and when trains came in, he pulled the empty coaches away so that the big engines could have a rest.

But what Thomas really wanted was his very own branch line. That way he would be a Really Useful Engine.

Thomas was a cheeky little engine. He thought no engine worked as hard as he did, and he liked playing tricks on the others.

One day, Gordon had just returned from pulling the big Express. He was very tired, and had just gone to sleep when Thomas came up beside him:

"WAKE UP, LAZYBONES!" whistled Thomas. "Do some hard work for a change!" And he steamed off, laughing.

Gordon got a terrible shock. He decided he had to pay Thomas back.

The next morning, Thomas wouldn't wake up. His Driver and Fireman couldn't make him start.

It was nearly time for Gordon's Express to leave. Gordon was waiting, but Thomas hadn't got his coaches ready.

At last Thomas started. "Oh dear! Oh dear!" he yawned.

"Poop! Poop! Poop! Hurry up, you!" said Gordon crossly.

"Peep! Peep! Peep! Hurry up yourself!" replied Thomas, cheekily.

Thomas usually pushed behind Gordon's train to help him start. But he was always uncoupled first, so that when the train was running nicely Thomas could stop and go back.

That morning, Gordon saw the perfect chance to pay Thomas back for giving him a fright. He started so quickly that the Guards forgot to uncouple Thomas.

Gordon moved slowly out of the station, pulling the train and Thomas with him. Then he started to go faster and faster – much too fast for Thomas!

"Peep! Peep! Stop! Stop!" whistled Thomas.

"Hurry, hurry, hurry, hurry!" laughed Gordon in front.

You can't get away. You can't get away," giggled the coaches.

Poor Thomas was going faster than he had ever gone before.

"I shall never be the same again," he thought, sadly. "My wheels will be quite worn out."

At last they stopped at a station. Thomas was uncoupled and given a long, long drink.

"Well, little Thomas," chuckled Gordon. "Now you know what hard work means, don't you?"

Poor Thomas was too breathless to answer.

The next day, Thomas was working in the Yard. On a siding by themselves were some strange-looking trucks.

"That's the breakdown train," said his Driver. "When there's an accident, the workmen use it to help clear and mend the line."

Just then, James came whistling through the Yard crying, "Help! Help!" His brake blocks were on fire and his trucks were pushing him faster and faster.

James disappeared into the distance.

Soon after, a bell rang in the signal box and a man came running.

"James is off the line! We need the breakdown train – quickly!" he shouted.

Thomas was coupled on to the breakdown train, and off he went as fast as he could.

"Bother those trucks and their tricks!" he said. "I hope James isn't hurt."

They found James and the trucks at a bend in the line. James was in a field, with a cow staring at him. The brake van and the last few trucks were still on the rails, but the front ones were piled in a heap behind James.

James' Driver and Fireman were checking to see if he was hurt.

"Don't worry, James," his Driver said. "It wasn't your fault – it was those Troublesome Trucks."

Thomas pushed the breakdown train alongside James, then he pulled the
trucks that were still on the line out of the way.

"Oh . . . dear! Oh . . . dear!" they groaned.

"Serves you right. Serves you right," puffed Thomas, crossly.

As soon as the other trucks were back on the line, Thomas pulled them
away, too. He was hard at work all afternoon.

Using two cranes, the men put James carefully back on the rails. He tried to
move, but he couldn't, so Thomas pulled him back to the shed.

The Fat Controller was waiting for them there.

"Well, Thomas," he said kindly, "I've heard all about it and I think you're
a Really Useful Engine. I'm so pleased with you, that I'm going to give you
your own branch line."

"Oh, thank you, Sir!" said Thomas, happily.

Now Thomas is as content as can be. He has a branch line all to himself, and he puffs proudly backwards and forwards from morning till night, with his coaches Annie and Clarabel.

Edward and Henry stop quite often at the junction to talk to him.

Gordon is always in a hurry and does not stop, but he never forgets to say, "Poop! Poop! Poop!" to Thomas; and Thomas always whistles, "Peep! Peep! Peep!" in return.

Bertie and the Great Race

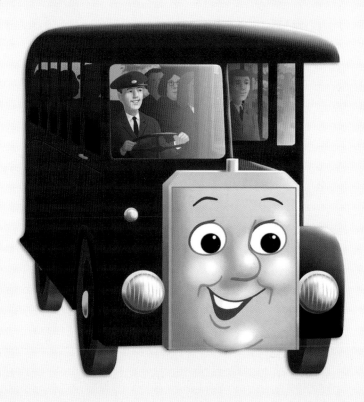

This is a story about Bertie the Bus. Bertie and Thomas both think they can go fastest.

They just can't agree, so they decide to have a race to settle the argument once and for all . . .

One day, Thomas was waiting at the junction when a bus came into the yard.

"Hello," said Thomas. "Who are you?"

"I'm Bertie. Who are you?"

"I'm Thomas. I run this branch line."

"Ah – I remember now," said Bertie. "You were stuck in the snow. I took your passengers, and Terence the Tractor pulled you out. I've come to help you with your passengers today."

"Help me?" said Thomas crossly. "I don't need any help. Anyway, I can go faster than you."

"You can't," said Bertie.

"I can," huffed Thomas.

"I'll race you," said Bertie.

Their drivers agreed to the race. "Are you ready?" asked the Stationmaster. "Then, *go*!" And they were off . . .

Thomas always had to start off slowly, and Bertie was soon ahead of him.
But Thomas didn't hurry.

"Why don't you go fast? Why don't you go fast?" called Annie and
Clarabel, anxiously.

"Wait and see! Wait and see!" hissed Thomas.

"He's a long way ahead, a long way ahead," they wailed.

But Thomas didn't mind. He remembered the level crossing.

Bertie was there, waiting impatiently at the gates while Thomas and his carriages went sailing through.

"Goodbye, Bertie," called Thomas.

After that, the road left the railway, so Thomas, Annie and Clarabel couldn't see Bertie. Then they had to stop at a station to let some passengers off.

"Peep, pip, peep! Quickly, please!" called Thomas.

Everybody got out quickly, the Guard blew his whistle and off they went again.

"Come along. Come along," sang Thomas.

"We're coming along. We're coming along!" sang Annie and Clarabel.

"Hurry! Hurry! Hurry!" panted Thomas.

Then he looked ahead and saw Bertie crossing the bridge over the railway, tooting triumphantly on his horn!

"Oh, deary me! Oh, deary me!" groaned Thomas.

"Steady, Thomas," said his Driver. "We'll beat Bertie yet."

"We'll beat Bertie yet. We'll beat Bertie yet," echoed Annie and Clarabel.

"We'll do it. We'll do it," panted Thomas. "Oh, bother, there's a station!"

As Thomas stopped, he heard a toot.

"Goodbye, Thomas," called Bertie. "You must be tired. Sorry I can't stop – we buses have to work, you know. Goodbye!"

The next station was by the river. They got there quickly, but the signal was up.

"Oh, dear," thought Thomas. "We've lost!"

But at the station he had a drink of water and felt much better.

Then the signal dropped: "Hurrah, we're off! Hurrah, we're off!" puffed Thomas happily.

As Thomas crossed the bridge, he heard an impatient, "Toot! Toot!"

There was Bertie, waiting at the traffic lights.

But as soon as the lights changed, Bertie started with a roar, and chased after Thomas.

Now Thomas reached his full speed. Bertie tried hard, but Thomas was too fast.

Whistling joyfully, he plunged into the tunnel, leaving Bertie far behind.

"I've done it. I've done it," panted Thomas.

"We've done it, hooray! We've done it, hooray!" chanted Annie and Clarabel, as they whooshed into the last station.

The passengers all cheered loudly. When Bertie came in, they also gave him a big welcome.

"Well done, Thomas," said Bertie. "That was fun, but I would have to grow wings like an aeroplane to beat you over that hill!"

Thomas and Bertie now keep each other busy. Bertie finds people who want to travel by train and takes them to Thomas, while Thomas brings people to the station for Bertie to take home.

They often talk about their race. But Bertie's passengers don't like being bounced around like peas in a pan, and The Fat Controller has told Thomas not to race at dangerous speeds.

So although they would like to have another race, Bertie and Thomas have agreed not to . . . until the next time!

Cranky and the Big Storm

This is a story about Cranky the Crane.
He worked at the Docks on the Island of Sodor.

He played tricks on the engines, to get them
into trouble. But one day Cranky needed
the engines' help . . .

Thomas and Percy liked working at the Docks. So when The Fat Controller told them they would be working there for two weeks, they could hardly wait.

When they arrived at the Docks, there was a new crane there called Cranky.

Cranky was always moody and he called Thomas and Percy 'useless little bugs'.

The two engines were very upset. They told Gordon and James about how rude Cranky had been. To their surprise, James and Gordon backed up Cranky.

"He's so high up in the air," said James, "facing the wind, rain and sunshine, that it's no wonder he looks down and sees you as annoying little bugs!"

Thomas and Percy hoped Cranky would stop being so mean to them.

The next day, Cranky played a trick on Thomas. He told him to move the trucks to the outer track. Thomas was surprised, but he did as he was told.

When The Fat Controller arrived, Cranky said, "I asked Thomas to put those trucks on the inner track, but he has put them on the outer track, where I can't reach them. And Percy won't do as he's told, either!"

The Fat Controller was furious. He sent the engines back to the station in disgrace. Thomas and Percy were shocked. Cranky was making it all up!

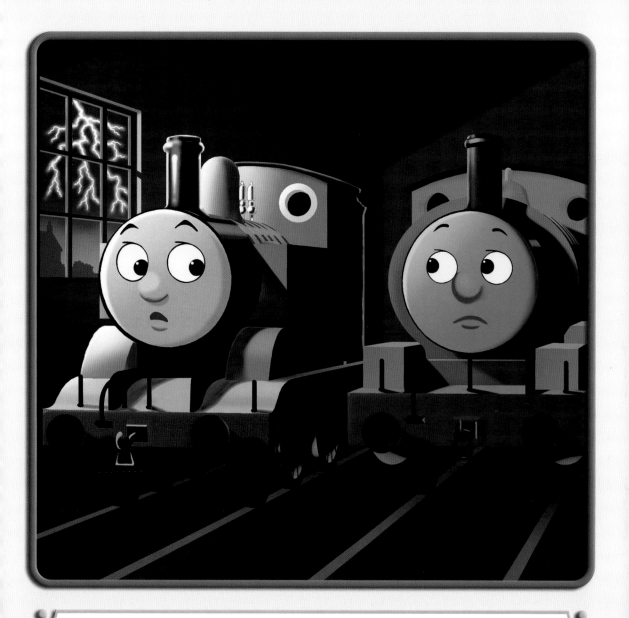

A storm raged across the Island of Sodor that night.

At The Fat Controller's station, Thomas and Percy talked about Cranky. They were upset that The Fat Controller had believed his lies. They wondered if they'd ever be allowed to work at the Docks again.

"If Cranky is going to continue being nasty to us then I don't want to work at the Docks anyway!" Thomas said.

Percy had to agree.

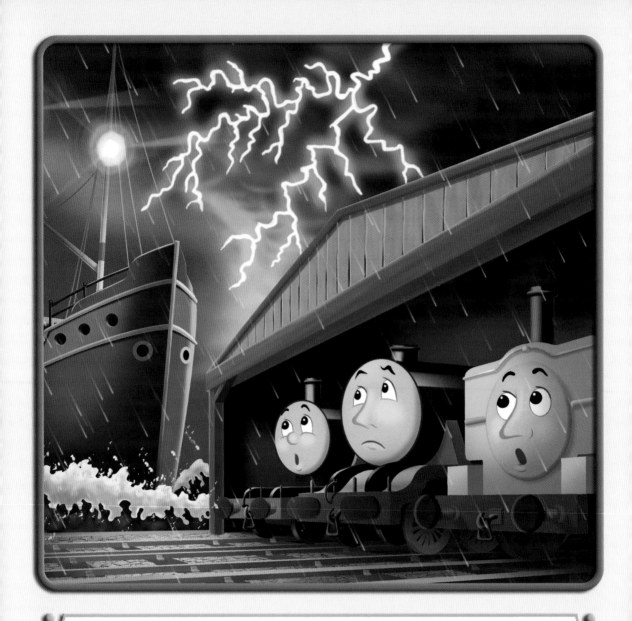

At the Docks, wind and rain were lashing down on Cranky. He wasn't worried though – he thought he was much stronger than any storm.

In the shed near by, Duck, James and Gordon were listening to the storm. They thought they were safe there, but they were wrong. A huge steamer had got loose and it was heading straight for the Docks!

The steamer ran aground. It charged through the Docks, crashing into the shed and knocking over Cranky.

Duck, Gordon and James were trapped! They called to Cranky for help but Cranky had fallen on to his side, so he needed rescuing, too!

Cranky and the engines had to wait for the storm to clear before they could be rescued.

The next morning, The Fat Controller went to the Docks.

"Thomas and Percy are coming to help you, Cranky," he said. "They'll have you up again in no time!"

"Oh, thank you!" said Cranky. "Erm, can you tell them I'm sorry that I was so mean to them?"

"So it was you that was causing all the trouble?" said The Fat Controller. "It seems I owe those engines an apology."

Thomas and Percy's Drivers tied ropes to Cranky and attached them to the engines. Thomas and Percy quickly pulled Cranky back upright.

Cranky was very glad to see the world the right way up again. He got straight to work, clearing away the rubble.

Cranky moved the steamer back into the water and it was carefully tied in place. Then it was safe for him to pull the heavy rubble away from the shed so the trapped engines could get out.

Duck, Gordon and James were very grateful. They had not liked being stuck in the shed.

They thanked Cranky for his help.

Cranky told them Thomas and Percy had rescued him first.

"I never thought I'd be rescued by a couple of . . ." Cranky was about to say 'bugs', but he stopped himself just in time.

"Erm," he continued, "I never thought I would be saved by a couple of small engines! I'll try not to be rude to you again."

Thomas and Percy smiled. They were just about to reply when Cranky said, "Now move out of the way, you mites, I need to get to those trucks!"

"Pah!" said Percy. "Cranky wasn't polite for long – he's back to bugging us!"

Percy quickly moved up the track to get out of Cranky's way, but he had forgotten that his ropes were still attached to Cranky.

"Wait!" cried Thomas, but he was too late. As Percy charged forward, the ropes pulled taut and Cranky crashed back to the ground with a THUMP!

Thomas and Percy had to pull Cranky up for the second time. Cranky felt very silly.

Now Cranky works well with Thomas and Percy. He still looks down on them from his high perch in the sky, but he never calls them bugs or mites. After that stormy night, he knows they can be Really Useful Engines; after all, they had rescued him twice!

And if Cranky is ever knocked over again, he knows the little engines will quickly put him back in his place.

Gordon and the Faulty Whistle

This is a story about Gordon the Big Engine.
He was a very proud engine who always
thought he knew best.

But then one day something happened to
make him realise otherwise . . .

Gordon was always boasting and telling the other engines how to behave.

One day, he was showing off to Edward. "You watch me this afternoon as I rush through with the Express," he said. "That will be a splendid sight for you when you're shunting trucks."

And before he puffed away, Gordon continued, "Don't play around with the trucks, Edward. It isn't wrong, but we just don't do it."

Edward ignored Gordon. It was fun playing with the trucks. He came up quietly behind them and gave them a push. Then he stopped suddenly and the silly trucks bumped into each other.

"Ooh!" they cried. "Whatever is happening?"

Edward played until there were no more trucks to move. Then he stopped to rest.

Suddenly, Edward heard a whistle. It was Gordon, and he was very cross.

Instead of pulling nice shiny coaches, he was pulling lots of dirty coal trucks!

"A Goods Train!" he grumbled. "The shame of it!"

Gordon went slowly past, with the trucks clattering behind him.

Edward laughed, and went to find more trucks.

But soon there was trouble. A Porter came and spoke to Edward's Driver.

"Gordon can't get up the hill," he said. "Will you take Edward to push him, please?"

Edward found Gordon halfway up the hill. His Driver was very cross with him.

"You are not trying!" he shouted at Gordon.

"I can't do it," replied Gordon. "The silly coal trucks are holding me back."

Edward came up behind Gordon's brake van, ready to push.

"You'll be no use at all," huffed Gordon.

"You wait and see," replied Edward.

The Guard blew his whistle and Gordon tried to pull forward as Edward pushed him as hard as he could.

"I can't do it, I can't do it, I can't do it," puffed Gordon.

"I will do it, I will do it, I will do it," puffed Edward.

Edward pushed and puffed with all his strength. And before long, Gordon was at the top of the hill.

"I've done it!" he said proudly, forgetting all about Edward, pushing behind. And Gordon ran on to the next station without stopping to say 'thank you'.

But The Fat Controller didn't forget to thank Edward. The next day, he was given a beautiful coat of blue paint with red stripes.

Gordon hadn't learnt his lesson. He still boasted and told the other engines how to behave. Now it was Henry's turn.

"Henry whistles too much," said Gordon. "Respectable engines don't whistle loudly at stations. It isn't wrong, but we just don't do it."

Poor Henry felt sad.

"Never mind," whispered Percy, "I like your whistling."

The next morning, as Gordon left the shed, he called to Henry:

"Goodbye Henry, be sure and remember what I said about whistling."

Later that day, Henry took a slow train to Edward's station.

"Hello, Henry," said Edward. "I was pleased to hear your happy whistle yesterday."

"Thank you, Edward," smiled Henry. "Shh! Can you hear something?"

Edward listened. Far away, but getting louder and louder, was the sound of an engine's whistle.

"It sounds like Gordon," said Edward. "But Gordon never whistles like that."

But it was Gordon. He came rushing down the hill at a tremendous speed.

Gordon's whistle valve wouldn't close and he was whistling fit to burst.

He screamed through the station and disappeared.

"Well!" said Edward, looking at Henry.

"It isn't wrong, but we just don't do it," chuckled Henry, and Edward laughed.

Meanwhile, Gordon screeched along the line. People came out of their houses, fire engines set off to find the fire, and old ladies dropped their parcels in shock. The noise was awful. Porters and passengers held their ears. The Fat Controller held his ears, too.

"Take him away," he bellowed. "And stop that noise!" Still whistling, Gordon puffed sadly away.

He whistled as he crossed the points. He whistled in the siding. Gordon was still whistling as the last passenger left the station!

Then two Fitters climbed up and knocked Gordon's whistle valve into place. And at last there was silence.

Gordon slunk into the shed. He was very glad it was empty. He didn't want anyone to make fun of him.

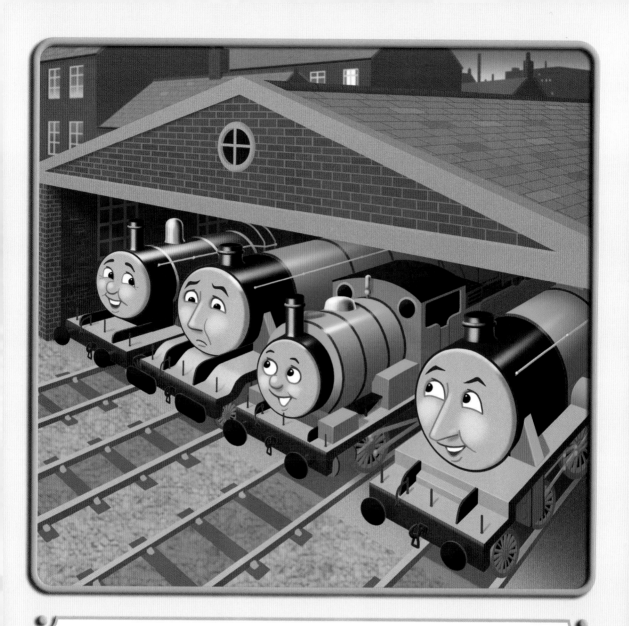

Later that evening, the other engines came back.

"It isn't wrong," murmured Edward, "but we just don't do it."

And all the engines laughed, apart from Gordon.

From then on, Gordon was a much quieter, humbler engine – well, for a few days, anyway!

The Fat Controller
and the
New Tank Engine

This is a story about Sir Topham Hatt,
or The Fat Controller as his engines call him.

He has loved trains ever since he was a boy
but engines are sometimes as troublesome
as trucks . . .

One morning, The Fat Controller was eating his usual breakfast of toast and marmalade. Lady Hatt was just pouring him a cup of coffee, when the telephone rang.

"Bother that telephone!" said The Fat Controller, frowning.

"I'm sorry, my dear," he said to Lady Hatt, a few minutes later. "The engines are not behaving themselves, I must go at once. Engines on my Railway do as they are told!"

When he arrived at the Main Station, there was a tremendous noise.
The passengers waiting on the platform were angry.

   The Fat Controller went into his office and sat down behind his desk.
Moments later, the Stationmaster knocked on the door.

   "There's trouble in the shed, Sir," he said. "Henry is sulking. There's no train
and the passengers are saying this is a bad Railway."

   "Indeed," said The Fat Controller. "We cannot allow that."

At the sheds, The Fat Controller found Gordon, James and Henry looking very cross.

"Come along, Henry. It's time your train was ready," said The Fat Controller.

"Henry's not going," said Gordon. "We won't shunt like common tank engines. That is Thomas' job."

"We are important tender engines. Fetch our coaches and we will pull them. Tender engines don't shunt!" huffed Henry.

"Oh, indeed," said The Fat Controller. "We'll see about that. Engines on my Railway do as they are told."

And he hurried away in his car to find Edward.

"The Yard has not been the same since Thomas left to run his branch line," he thought sadly, as he took out his handkerchief to mop his brow.

Meanwhile, Edward was shunting.

"Leave those trucks, please, Edward," said The Fat Controller. "I want you to push coaches for me in the Yard."

"Thank you, Sir, that will be a nice change," said Edward, happily.

"That's a good engine, off you go then," replied The Fat Controller.

So Edward found coaches for Gordon, James and Henry, and that day the trains ran as usual.

But the next morning, Edward looked unhappy. Gordon came clanking past, hissing rudely.

"Bless me," said The Fat Controller. "What a noise!"

"They all hiss at me, Sir," sighed Edward. "They say tender engines don't shunt and that I have dirty wheels like the trucks. I haven't, have I, Sir?"

"You have nice blue ones, Edward," said The Fat Controller, kindly. "Tender engines do shunt, but we need another tank engine here."

The Fat Controller went to the Workshop and inspected all sorts of engines. At last, he saw a little green tank engine with four wheels.

"That's the one," he thought. The Fat Controller knew a Really Useful Engine when he saw one. "If I choose you, will you work hard?" he said.

"Oh, Sir. Yes, Sir!" peeped the little green engine.

"That's a good engine. I'll call you Percy," smiled The Fat Controller. And he drove him all the way back to the Yard.

"Edward . . ." he called, "here's Percy. Will you show him what to do?"

Percy soon learned what needed doing, and he and Edward had a happy afternoon.

Then Henry steamed by, hissing as usual.

But: "Wheeeesh!" – little Percy hissed back!

Henry was so surprised, he almost jumped off the track!

The next day, The Fat Controller arrived. Edward, Thomas and Percy were excited.

He told the engines that Henry, Gordon and James were sulking:

"They refuse to shunt like 'common tank engines', so I have shut them in the shed. I want you to run the line for a while," he said.

"Common tank engines, indeed!" snorted Thomas. "We'll show them."

"And Percy will help, too," continued The Fat Controller.

"Thank you, Sir!" whistled Percy, with delight.

Edward and Thomas worked the Main Line, peep-peeping to each other as they passed by.

Percy puffed along the Branch Line, carrying passengers to their stations.

Thomas was worried about Annie and Clarabel, but his Driver and Guard promised to look after them.

There were fewer trains, but the passengers didn't mind. They knew the three naughty engines were being taught a lesson.

In the shed, Gordon, James and Henry were cold, lonely and miserable.

There was no coal for them, no washdown and they missed their passengers.

They wished they hadn't been so silly.

The next morning, The Fat Controller visited the shed. He could see that the engines had learned their lesson.

"We are sorry, Sir," said Gordon.

"We were too big for our buffers!" added James.

"Remember, only Really Useful Engines can work on my Railway!" said The Fat Controller. He knew just how to handle difficult engines.

And the three tender engines were never rude to tank engines again.

Toby and the Lucky Escape

This is a story about Toby the Tram Engine.
Toby loved people, but everyone thought
he was too old-fashioned.

He felt very sad, until one day someone
came to his rescue …

Toby was a Tram Engine. He had cow catchers and side plates, and a coach called Henrietta. Toby loved people and was always happy when he could help them out. He was such a cheerful engine that people liked to help him, too.

Toby and Henrietta worked on a little line near a holiday town. They worked very hard, taking trucks from the farms to the Main Line. But they had very few passengers.

"It's not fair!" grumbled Henrietta, one day. "The buses are always full of passengers, even though they often have accidents. We never have accidents, but I have hardly any passengers."

"I can't understand it," said Toby, feeling sad.

Sometimes the people on the buses laughed at Toby and called him old-fashioned. This made Toby cross.

One day, a car stopped near by and two children jumped out.

"Come and look at this engine!" called the little boy.

A nice-looking stout gentleman followed them with two ladies.

"That's a tram engine," explained the stout gentleman. "It's a special kind of steam train."

"Can we have a ride in it?" asked the little girl.

They all climbed into Henrietta and the Guard blew his whistle. Toby set off, feeling proud to have passengers.

"Hip, hip, hurray!" sang Henrietta as she rattled along. The stout gentleman and his family enjoyed their ride.

"Thank you, Toby," they said.

"Peep! Peep!" whistled Toby in reply. "Come again soon!"

"We will!" called the family, and they waved goodbye.

As time passed, Toby and Henrietta had fewer and fewer trucks to take to the Main Line, and they had no passengers at all.

One morning, the Driver looked very sad. "It's our last day, Toby," he said. "The Manager says we must close tomorrow."

At the end of the day Toby puffed slowly to his shed. "Nobody wants me," he said, unhappily.

But the next morning Toby had a big surprise! A letter had arrived for his Driver.

"It's from the stout gentleman," said the Driver. "Do you remember him, Toby?"

"I remember him very well," said Toby. "He knew how to speak to engines."

"No wonder," said his Driver. "That gentleman was The Fat Controller!"

The Fat Controller needed extra help on his Railway, and he had thought of the nice little engine he met on holiday. Toby could hardly believe it!

Toby and Henrietta set off that day. They were very excited. When they arrived at Tidmouth Sheds, The Fat Controller came to meet them.

"Thank you very much for asking me to come, Sir!" said Toby.

"I'm glad you're here, Toby!" said The Fat Controller. "I hope you will work hard and be a Useful Engine, just like Thomas."

"I'll try, Sir!" said Toby.

Thomas came up to say 'hello'. He showed Toby what to do and they were soon very good friends.

Toby loved working on The Fat Controller's Railway and he soon learned to be a Really Useful Engine.

Next to Thomas' branch line was a cottage. The lady who lived there liked to see Toby and Thomas puffing past. She always waved to them from her window.

"That is Mrs Kyndley," Thomas told Toby. "She isn't very well, and she has to stay in bed all day."

"Poor lady," said Toby. "I wish we could help her." From then on, Toby and Thomas always whistled to Mrs Kyndley when they passed her cottage.

One day, it was raining hard as Thomas hurried along the track with Toby following behind. Suddenly, Thomas' Driver pointed at Mrs Kyndley's cottage.

"Something's wrong!" he said, for a big red cloth was waving out of the cottage window.

"Perhaps Mrs Kyndley needs help!" said Thomas' Fireman.

Thomas stopped carefully, just before a bend in the track.

Thomas' Driver and Fireman hurried to the cottage. But when they looked around the bend, they understood why Mrs Kyndley had stopped them.

"A landslide!" said the Driver. "Mrs Kyndley has saved our lives!"

Mrs Kyndley had seen the landslide, and had waved her red dressing gown out of the window, to warn the engines.

The line was cleared the next day, and a very special train puffed along the branch line towards Mrs Kyndley's cottage. First came Toby, then Thomas with Annie and Clarabel, and last of all came Henrietta. The Fat Controller was there, too.

Everyone wanted to say 'thank you' to Mrs Kyndley.

When they reached the bend in the track they stopped. The people got out and climbed up to the cottage. Toby and Thomas wished they could go, too!

Thomas' Driver gave Mrs Kyndley a new dressing gown. The Guard gave her some grapes and Toby and Thomas sent some coal as a present.

"The engines and I would like to give you these tickets for a trip to the seaside," said The Fat Controller. "We hope you will get better in the sunshine!"

"You are very kind!" said Mrs Kyndley.

Toby and Thomas blew their whistles to say 'thank you'! Toby felt very happy that he had come to work on The Fat Controller's Railway.

"Hip, hip, hurray!" sang Henrietta!

Henry and the Special Coal

This is a story about Henry the Green Engine.
Henry was often ill and couldn't work.

But then he tried some special Welsh coal,
and got the chance to show everyone just
what he could do …

Henry was a big engine. Sometimes he could pull trains, but sometimes he felt too weak, and had to stay in the yard.

One morning, Henry was feeling very sorry for himself: "I suffer dreadfully, and no one cares," he said.

"Rubbish, Henry," snorted James. "You don't work hard enough!"

The Fat Controller spoke to Henry:

"You're too expensive, Henry," he said. "You have had lots of new parts and a new coat of paint, but they have done you no good. If we can't make you better, we will have to get another engine instead of you."

This made Henry, his Driver and his Fireman very sad.

The Fat Controller was waiting when Henry arrived at the platform the next morning.

He had taken off his hat and coat and put on overalls, and now he climbed onto Henry's footplate.

Henry managed to start, but his Fireman was not happy.

"Henry is a bad steamer," he told The Fat Controller. "I build up his fire, but it doesn't give enough heat."

Henry tried very hard to pull the train, but it was no good. He didn't have enough steam.

He gradually came to a stop outside Edward's station.

"Oh dear," thought Henry. "Now I shall be sent away. Oh dear. Oh dear."

He went slowly into a siding, and Edward took charge of the train.

"What do you think is wrong, Fireman?" asked The Fat Controller.

"It's the coal, Sir," the Fireman answered. "It hasn't been very good lately. The other engines can manage because they have big fireboxes, but Henry's is small and can't make enough heat. With Welsh coal, though, he'd be a different engine."

"It's expensive," said The Fat Controller, "but Henry must have a fair chance. I'll send James to fetch some."

Henry's Driver and Fireman were very excited when the coal came.

"Now we'll show them, Henry, old fellow," they said.

They carefully oiled Henry's joints, and polished his brass until it shone like gold. Henry felt very proud.

Then Henry's Fireman carefully made his fire. He put large lumps of coal like a wall around the outside of the fire. Then he covered the glowing middle part with smaller lumps.

"You're spoiling my fire," complained Henry.

"Wait and see," said the Fireman. "We'll have a roaring fire just when we need it."

The Fireman was right. When Henry reached the platform, the water was boiling nicely, and he had to let off steam. "Wheeesh!"

"How are you, Henry?" asked The Fat Controller.

"Peep! Peep! Peep!" whistled Henry. "I feel fine!"

"Do you have a good fire, Driver?" The Fat Controller asked.

"Never better, Sir, and plenty of steam," the Driver replied.

Henry was impatient. He wanted to set off.

"No record breaking," warned The Fat Controller. "Don't push him too hard, Driver."

"Henry won't need pushing, Sir," the Driver replied. "I'll have to hold him back!"

Henry had a lovely day. He had never felt so well in his life. He wanted to go fast, but his Driver wouldn't let him.

"Steady, old fellow," he said. "There's plenty of time."

But still, Henry went quite fast, and they arrived at the station early. Thomas puffed in.

"Where have you been, lazybones?" asked Henry.

But before Thomas could answer, Henry was off again. "I can't wait for slow tank engines like you," he said. "Goodbye!" And off he sped.

"Gosh!" said Thomas to Annie and Clarabel. "Have you ever seen anything like it?" Annie and Clarabel agreed that they never had.

Henry was very happy. With his new Welsh coal, he could work as hard as the other engines.

Then, one day, Henry had a crash and The Fat Controller sent him to be mended. Workmen gave Henry a brand new shape, and a bigger firebox, so he wouldn't need special coal any more.

Now Henry is so splendid and strong, he sometimes pulls the Express!

"Peep! Peep! Pippippeep!" whistles Henry happily.

Daisy and the Lesson Learnt

This is a story about Daisy the Diesel Railcar.
She worked for The Fat Controller while
Thomas was being repaired.

She was bossy and thought she always knew
best, but she soon learnt
not to be so bullish . . .

One day, when Thomas was being repaired, The Fat Controller brought Daisy to work at the station.

"Look at me!" she said to the passengers. "I'm highly sprung and right up to date. After travelling with me, you won't want to ride in Thomas' bumpy carriages again!"

The passengers climbed aboard and waited for Daisy to set off.

Every morning, milk was collected from the farms and put on a wagon at the station. The wagon was coupled to Thomas' first train of the day, so he could take it to the Dairy. That day, the milk wagon was waiting for Daisy.

"I won't take that!" she said, in horror.

"Nonsense," said her Driver. "Come on now, it won't take long."

But Daisy refused to move.

Daisy lied so she wouldn't have to take the wagon.

"My Fitter says I'm highly sprung and pulling is bad for my swerves," she said.

"I can't understand it," said a workman. "Whatever made The Fat Controller send us such a feeble –"

"F-f-f-feeble?" spluttered Daisy, crossly.

"Stop arguing!" cried the passengers. "We're already late."

Nothing Daisy's Driver or Guard said would change her mind, so workmen moved the milk wagon and Daisy went smugly on her way.

"I made up a clever story," she chuckled to herself. "Now I can do the jobs I want to do and no more!"

When Toby came to the station, he was surprised to see the milk wagon there.

"Daisy's left the milk," Percy said, crossly. "Now I'll have to make a special journey with it and I'm already late for the Quarry."

"Why don't I take the milk to the Dairy and you fetch my Quarry trucks?" Toby said. "That way we can both save time."

It was agreed and both engines set off.

A little later, Toby met Daisy at a junction. She laughed at his side plates and cow catchers. Toby explained that he had them to stop animals being hurt if they got on to the track in front of him.

"You're just scared!" Daisy said, rudely. "If I see an animal on the track, I'll toot and it will move!"

"I'm not scared," Toby replied, calmly. "And they won't just move if you toot!"

"They will for me," said Daisy, proudly.

When Daisy reached the next station, a policeman waved for her to stop.

"Champion the bull is on the track," he said. "Please move him along to the farmer."

"I'll show Toby how to manage animals," Daisy said to her Driver.

But she was about to be surprised . . .

"Move on!" tooted Daisy when she saw the bull, but Champion didn't move.

After a while, he became curious and slowly walked towards Daisy.

"Ooh!" said Daisy, nervously. "Look at his big horns. If I bump into them, he might hurt – er – himself."

She quickly backed away and left.

Meanwhile, Percy had picked up Toby's trucks. He was still grumpy about Daisy, so he was rude to the trucks. The trucks decided to teach him a lesson.

As he pulled them over a big hill, they shoved him forward, sending him racing out of control.

"Help!" Percy cried as he flew through a level crossing, and crashed into some stone trucks in the yard.

Toby was leaving the station when Daisy crept back. One of her passengers told him what had happened.

"Now you know why my side plates and cow catchers are so useful!" Toby chuckled.

Just then, a workman told them about Percy's crash.

"If you help Percy," Toby said to Daisy, "I'll take your passengers and move the bull."

Daisy agreed and both engines set off.

Daisy worked hard all afternoon. She moved all the stone trucks away from the track, so the breakdown train could rescue Percy.

The Fat Controller came to speak to Daisy.

"I heard that you left the milk wagon," he said, crossly. "I won't have lazy engines working on my Railway! However, you have done a good job here so, if you promise to work hard and listen to the other engines, you can stay on."

"Thank you, Sir," said Daisy, humbly.

Thomas came back to work the next day. Daisy stayed on to help while Percy was being repaired. The Fat Controller was very pleased because she had worked hard and listened to the other engines.

Daisy became good friends with the engines and, sometimes, she even delivered the milk wagon for Thomas!

Diesel and the Oil Spill

This is a story about Diesel the Diesel Engine.
He played tricks on other engines, so no one
liked working with him.

But when Thomas got into trouble,
would Diesel come to his rescue?

One day, Percy wasn't feeling well. His joints ached and he couldn't breathe properly. The Fat Controller came to inspect him.

"You need to go to the Works to be repaired," he said. "I'll have to get another engine to do your work until you're better."

The Fat Controller phoned other Railways to see if anyone could spare an engine. But the only available engine was Diesel.

    The Fat Controller didn't want to use Diesel because the last time he had worked at his station, he had caused so much trouble that he had been sent away in disgrace. But, as no other engine could help out, Diesel had to do.

The next day, Diesel came to the station to collect the Troublesome Trucks.

Thomas was not happy to see him because Diesel had played so many tricks on him before.

"Take these trucks to the Harbour," Thomas said. "But don't play any silly tricks!" he warned him.

"Yes, Thomas. Of course I won't play tricks. I'll do whatever I'm told," Diesel said, slyly.

The Troublesome Trucks teased Diesel.

"Yes, Thomas. Of course I won't play tricks. I'll do whatever I'm told," they said, in Diesel's voice.

Diesel was angry. "I'll teach you!" he roared, and bumped into them roughly, sending them flying into a siding.

The trucks crashed through the buffers and slid off the track!

Diesel hadn't meant the trucks to crash, he had only wanted to scare them.

But, he still wanted them to do as they were told, so he said, "That will teach you to laugh at me!"

The Fat Controller was disappointed with Diesel.

"You will go back to the Other Railway as soon as I can arrange it," he said, sternly. "I won't have trouble on my Railway!"

After such a severe telling-off, Diesel was glad to be going home.

A few days later, Daisy was going up a hill when she felt something splash against her wheels. When she stopped at the next station, she felt hot and her joints were stiff.

"You've lost your oil," her Driver said. "Bertie can take your passengers while we get you repaired."

Thomas had to go over the hill where Daisy had spilt her oil. He was halfway up when his wheels started slipping on the oil.

Suddenly, Thomas, Annie and Clarabel slipped back down the hill. As they reached the bottom, Clarabel's wheels bounced off the main track on to an unfinished siding. Her front wheels fell off the end of the track and sank into the mud.

Thomas was left stranded across the main track.

Diesel was at the next station, waiting to go home. He laughed when he heard what had happened, but then he realised Thomas was blocking the track so he couldn't get past.

"Bother!" Diesel said, crossly. "I'll have to help Thomas or I can't get home."

Workmen cleaned the oil off the tracks. Then they put sand on them to help Diesel grip them. Diesel moved slowly forward and was coupled to Thomas.

Wooden railway sleepers were put under Clarabel's wheels, so she could be pulled back on to the rails.

"Thank you for coming to help, Diesel," said Thomas. "We could have been stuck here all day!"

Diesel gripped the sanded rails and pulled with all his strength. Slowly and carefully, he pulled Thomas, Annie and Clarabel back on to the main track.

"Well done, Diesel," said Thomas. "You have been a Really Useful Engine!"

Diesel smiled. It felt good to be helpful for a change instead of always causing trouble.

Diesel carefully pulled Thomas, Annie and Clarabel over the slippery hill and on to The Fat Controller's station.

"Good work, Diesel!" said The Fat Controller. "You've been so helpful today that I am happy for you to come back to work at my station!"

Diesel smiled. He was pleased that he was going home, but he was also glad that he could come back again to work for The Fat Controller!

Emily and the Black Loch Run

This is a story about Emily the Single Stirling Engine. When she came to the Railway, some of the engines were very unfriendly.

But they soon learnt that things are not always what they first appear to be . . .

A new engine was arriving on the Island of Sodor. Thomas puffed happily into Knapford Station. At the platform, there was a beautiful engine, with shiny paintwork and gleaming brass fittings.

"Thomas, meet Emily," said The Fat Controller.

"Hello," wheeshed Thomas. "Hello," puffed Emily.

"Emily, go and collect the coaches, so you can learn the passenger routes," said The Fat Controller.

"Yes, Sir," smiled Emily, and she steamed away.

The only coaches Emily could find were Annie and Clarabel. Her Driver hooked them up, and Emily puffed slowly and carefully along the track.
Annie and Clarabel grumbled all the way.

"There'll be trouble when Thomas finds out," whispered Clarabel.

But Emily couldn't understand why the coaches were so cross. She passed Edward and Percy and whistled a friendly hello. But the engines just stared angrily at her.

Emily was pleased to see Thomas puffing down the line.

"Hello, Thomas!" she called, cheerfully.

But Thomas glared at Emily when he saw she was pulling Annie and Clarabel.

"Those are *my* coaches!" he muttered, crossly.

Now Thomas was being rude, and Emily had no idea why. She chuffed away, feeling very sad.

Thomas was at Maithwaite Station when The Fat Controller arrived.

"I want you to go to the Docks to pick up some new coaches," he ordered.

"New coaches?" exclaimed Thomas. "But, Sir . . ."

"Really Useful Engines don't argue!" shouted The Fat Controller.

Thomas was very unhappy. He thought the new coaches were for him, and he wanted Annie and Clarabel back.

Later that day, Emily returned to the yard. Oliver was very surprised to see her pulling Annie and Clarabel.

"Those are Thomas' coaches!" he cried.

"No wonder he was cross," said Emily. "I will return them straight away."

Meanwhile, Thomas was puffing along the track with the new coaches. "Don't want new coaches," he chuffed, angrily.

Emily was on her way back when a Signalman waved her down. Oliver hadn't cleared his box! Emily sped off to see what was wrong.

Oliver had broken down on the track crossing, and his Driver had gone for help.

Suddenly, Emily heard a whistle in the distance. Thomas was steaming along the track, straight towards Oliver. He would never be able to stop in time! Emily quickly charged towards Oliver, and pushed him off the track, just before Thomas rocketed past!

Emily had saved Thomas and Oliver. That evening, The Fat Controller had a special surprise for her.

"Emily, you were a very brave engine!" he said. "So, it gives me great pleasure to present you with two brand new coaches!"

"Thank you, Sir!" replied Emily. "Thomas, I'm sorry I took Annie and Clarabel."

"And I'm sorry I was so cross," said Thomas.

Emily was very happy. She had two beautiful new coaches and a new friend.

Later that summer, The Fat Controller opened some new routes. Emily was given the Flour Mill Special.

"I have to do the Black Loch Run," huffed James.

"He's frightened of the Black Loch Monster," teased Thomas.

"Nonsense!" said James, and he puffed away.

"What's the Black Loch Monster?" asked Emily.

"Nobody knows," said Thomas. "Shapes move in the water, then disappear."

Emily was glad she didn't have to go to Black Loch.

The next morning, Emily collected the trucks from the flour mill. But they were being naughty. Emily pulled as hard as she could, but the trucks made her go very slowly. Emily was late delivering the flour, so there was no fresh bread that day.

The Fat Controller was cross. "I didn't have any toast for breakfast. If you are late again, you will have to do the Black Loch Run instead of James!"

"I must get the flour to the bakery on time tomorrow!" puffed Emily.

But the next day, the trucks were being naughty again. They told Emily to leave before they were coupled properly, so half of them were left behind.

The Bakery Manager was very angry when Emily arrived with only half the flour. Emily raced back to the mill for the rest of the trucks. She was very cross and shunted them with all her strength; but the trucks had taken their brakes off! They rolled backwards and splashed into the duck pond, and Emily was covered in a gluey, floury mess!

That evening, The Fat Controller came to see Emily. "You are going to take over the Black Loch Run!" he shouted.

"It might be nice," said Thomas, reassuringly. But Emily wasn't so sure.

The next morning, she puffed sadly to the station. There were lots of excited children and holidaymakers waiting for her.

"I mustn't let them down," she thought. And soon Emily was steaming up hills and through valleys.

Finally, Emily reached the murky waters of Black Loch. Suddenly, she saw something move in the water. Her boiler quivered and her valves rattled. Then the water settled, and Emily saw what the monster really was.

"It's a family of seals!" she cried, delightedly.

That evening, Emily took Thomas to watch the seals.

"Black Loch is a nice route after all," said Emily.

"Well, things aren't always what they seem!" said Thomas, cheerfully. And both engines smiled.

Donald and Douglas and The Fat Controller's Choice

This is a story about the twin Scottish engines, Donald and Douglas.

They both went to work at The Fat Controller's station, but he only needed one of them. Which one would he keep?

The Fat Controller's Railway was busier than ever. All the engines had to work very hard indeed.

"We don't know whether we're coming or going," grumbled Henry.

"I know you are working very hard," said The Fat Controller. "So I have arranged for a new engine, for goods work, to come from Scotland tomorrow."

But the next day, The Fat Controller got a surprise. Not one, but two engines arrived from Scotland! They were twins called Donald and Douglas, and they had lost their numbers. No one knew which of them was supposed to stay!

"One of you will have to go back to Scotland," said The Fat Controller. "I will paint numbers on you for now, but I will decide which is the better engine, and send the other one home."

So the engines were given new numbers. Donald was number nine and Douglas was number ten.

Donald and Douglas felt miserable. Neither of them wanted to stay without the other.

"We'll just have to be so well-behaved that he'll want to keep us both!" said Douglas.

"Aye!" said Donald. "He won't be able to choose between us!"

The twins enjoyed working on The Fat Controller's Railway. They were good at keeping the trucks in order, and they soon made friends with the other engines.

Every day, Gordon's Express train steamed in with a special coach for passengers travelling on Thomas' branch line. Duck had to remember to shunt the special coach for Thomas to pick up.

Douglas said to Duck, "Why don't I move the special coach tomorrow?"

"That would be very kind, Douglas," said Duck, gratefully.

The next day, when Gordon arrived with the special coach, Douglas was busy worrying about being sent back to Scotland.

"I couldn't abide going back alone," said Douglas to himself.

He was so worried that he forgot to take the special coach to Thomas. He pushed it into the siding and went to join Donald.

When Thomas came along, he couldn't find his coach. A group of angry passengers complained to The Fat Controller. The Fat Controller went to find Douglas.

"I'm very annoyed, Douglas," he said. "It looks as though you may be going back to Scotland!"

Next day, Douglas was extra careful and he didn't do anything wrong.

But Donald was unlucky. He backed into a siding where the rails were slippery. Poor Donald couldn't stop! He crashed through the buffers into a signal box, leaving the Signalman sitting on the coal in the tender!

"You clumsy great engine!" cried the Signalman. "You've jammed my points!"

The Fat Controller was very annoyed.

"I'm disappointed in you, Donald," he said. "I was going to send Douglas back and keep you, but now I'm not so sure!"

Donald felt very sorry.

That night, snow came to the Island and covered all the tracks. Most engines hate snow, but Donald and Douglas loved it! They knew just what to do.

They puffed busily backwards and forwards, patrolling the line. They even rescued other engines who had got stuck in the snow-drifts.

All the other engines liked Donald and Douglas. Everyone was sad that one of them was going to be sent away.

"They were wonderful in the snow," said Henry.

"What we need is a Deputation," said Edward.

"What is a Depotstation?" asked Henry.

"A Deputation is when engines tell The Fat Controller that something is wrong, and ask him to put it right," replied Edward.

It was decided that Percy should speak to The Fat Controller. He wished he didn't have to!

"Please, Sir, they've made me a Disputation," said Percy. "To speak to you, Sir."

"Do you mean a Deputation?" asked The Fat Controller, kindly.

"Yes, Sir. It's Donald and Douglas, Sir. Please don't send them away, Sir. They're nice engines, Sir."

The Fat Controller smiled.

The next day, The Fat Controller went to see Donald and Douglas.

"I hear you have been doing good work in the snow" he said. "What colour paint would you like?"

The twin engines stared at him. "Blue please, Sir," they said in surprise.

"Does this mean . . . we'll both be staying, Sir?" asked Donald.

"It certainly does!" said The Fat Controller.

But the rest of his speech was drowned in a delighted chorus of cheers and whistles!

Percy and the Solemn Promise

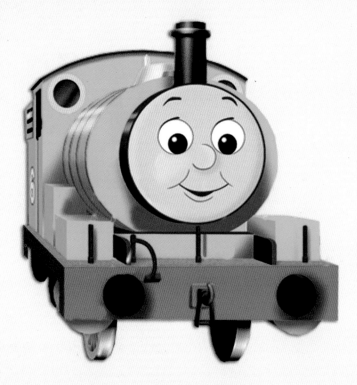

This is a story about Percy the little green
tank engine.

He was very cheeky and loved playing tricks
on the other engines. But one day
he needed to be brave . . .

Percy loved playing tricks on the other engines. But these tricks sometimes got him into trouble.

One morning he was being very cheeky indeed. "Peep, peep! Hurry up!" he whistled to Gordon. "Your Express train's ready."

Gordon thought he was late and came puffing out. But when he looked around there was only a train of dirty coal trucks!

"Ha, ha!" laughed Percy. But Gordon didn't think it was funny at all.

Next it was James' turn. Percy told James to stay in the shed because The Fat Controller was coming to see him.

James was a very proud engine, and thought that The Fat Controller must want him to pull a Special train. He stayed in the shed all day, and nothing his Driver could do would make him move.

The other engines were very annoyed. They had to do James' work as well as their own.

At last, The Fat Controller arrived. He was very cross with James. But he was even more angry with Percy when James explained what had happened.

When Percy arrived back at the Yard, The Fat Controller was waiting for him.

"You shouldn't waste time playing silly tricks, Percy!" shouted The Fat Controller. "You should be a Useful Engine."

Later that week, Thomas took the Sunday School children to the beach. As he was busy, he asked Percy if he could bring them home for him.

Percy thought that it sounded like very hard work. But he promised Thomas he would help.

The children had a lovely day. But by the afternoon, there were dark clouds overhead. Suddenly there was thunder and lightning, and the rain came lashing down! The children hurried to the station.

Annie and Clarabel were waiting for them at the platform. The children scrambled into the warm carriages.

"Percy, take the children home quickly, please," ordered the Stationmaster.

The rain poured down on Percy's boiler. "Ugh!" he shivered. He thought about pretending that he had broken down, so another engine would have to go instead of him. But then he remembered his promise. He must make sure the children got home safely.

Percy set off, bravely. But his Driver was worried. The rain was very heavy now and the river was rising fast.

The rain was getting in Percy's eyes and he couldn't see where he was going.

Suddenly he found himself in deep water. "Oooh, my wheels!" shivered Percy. But he struggled on.

"Oooshsh!" he hissed. The rain was beginning to put his fire out!

Percy's Driver decided to stop the train in a cutting. The Guard went to find a telephone. He returned looking very worried.

"We couldn't go back if we wanted to," he said. "The bridge near the junction is down."

They would have to carry on to the next station. But Percy's fire had nearly gone out, and they needed more wood to keep it going.

"We'll have to pull up the floorboards and burn them!" said the Fireman.

Soon they had plenty of wood. Percy's fire burned well and he felt warm and comfortable again.

Suddenly, there came a "Buzz! Buzz! Buzz!" Harold was flying overhead.

"Oh dear!" thought Percy, sadly. "Harold has come to laugh at me."

Bump! Something thudded on Percy's boiler. A parachute had landed on top of him! Harold hadn't come to laugh; he was dropping hot drinks! Everyone had a hot cocoa and felt much better.

Percy had got some steam up now.

"Peep! Peep! Thank you, Harold!" he whistled. "Come on, let's go!"

As Percy started to move, the water began to creep up and up and up.

It began to put his fire out again!

"Oooshsh!" shivered Percy.

Percy was losing steam, but he bravely carried on. "I promised Thomas," he panted. "I must keep my promise!"

The Fireman piled his fire high with wood. "I must do it," Percy gasped. "I must, I must, I must!"

Percy made a last great effort, and cleared the flood!

"Three cheers for Percy!" called the Vicar, and the children cheered as loudly as they could!

Harold arrived with The Fat Controller.

"Harold told me you were splendid, Percy," said The Fat Controller. "He says he can beat you at some things, but not at being a submarine! I don't know what you've both been doing, but I do know that you're a Really Useful Engine."

"Oh, thank you, Sir!" said Percy, happily.

The news of Percy's adventure soon got back to the Station.

Gordon and James heard all about how Percy had kept his promise and travelled through the terrible storm to bring the children home safely.

They both thought he was very brave and forgave him for all his tricks.

Percy realised that although playing tricks could be fun, it was much more important to be a Really Useful Engine!